Devious Desires

COLLECTION CONTAINING HONEY TRAP, FIREFIGHTER'S PET, AND DEMON LUST

NICOLINA MARTIN

Edited by Nerine Dorman

Cover by MethodMike

Introduction

In between the romance, I write my dirtiest, steamiest, craziest fantasies, and I'm happy to share them with you.

This boxset contains three erotica short stories.

Enjoy.

Part One

Honey Trap

I stand at the deserted bus station with my worn backpack next to my feet. Several of the nearby street lights are broken, and the ones that are still working sway back and forth in the wind. Light reflects in the puddles of rain on the uneven asphalt.

I'm an idiot for leaving. It's smarter to stay, even with an abusive father. I should finish high school, not run away with a few dollars in my pocket, and the clothes I can fit in my backpack. But my heart says anything has to be better than the hell I've endured since Mom left.

I peek out in the rain to check if the bus is coming. Nope, nothing but the empty street. I retreat under the roof of the shelter and wipe the wetness off my face. Why did I choose tonight of all nights? But I know why. My father has been unconscious after boozing the whole afternoon again. He would've come at me when he woke, and I can't take it anymore. The man hates me because I look like Mom. I hate him back because he's nothing but an abusive asshole, and because he's started looking at me as if I'm a woman. I have to leave. It can't wait even a few months.

The sound of an engine interrupts my musings and I glance up. The large silver Greyhound pulling in at the stop is one of the best things I've seen in a long while. As the door whizzes open, I grab my backpack and rush onboard. Something glints in the eyes of the driver as I fumble for my wallet. He stares at my breasts. They've grown during the past year, and I've gotten used to guys no longer meeting my pale blue eyes. Tonight I'm also Miss-Wet-Fucking-T-shirt. My nipples are showing as hard peaks through the fabric. I should've worn more than my tiny shorts and the T-shirt, but I didn't think. I grabbed whatever clothes and money I could find, pulled on my Doc Martens and ran while I had the chance. For all the shit my father's put me through over the years, I deserve whatever I stole from him. I have paid for a ride across the country, and there's not much left. I'll have to be careful how I spend the rest.

Freedom! Joy erupts in my chest at the realization. The door behind me whizzes closed, and with a firm grip on my bag I start down the aisle to find a seat as we start to move.

I'm so excited I can't wipe the grin off my face. I'm eighteen and my adult life is just starting. The world is mine.

A bitter-looking elderly couple glares at me as I pass. The man whispers something to the woman. Then the bus is empty save for a lone man sprawled across the seats in the rear, who appears to be asleep. In the dim light, with his ball cap pulled down over his face, his features are hidden. Fuck. Hopefully he'll get off soon, that's where I wanted to sit.

I throw my backpack into the overhead compartment in the middle of the bus and sink down on the seat under it. The hairs on my nape rise as if I'm being watched. I spin and glance back at the man. He hasn't moved. Okay. Fine. Whatever. Let him look.

* * *

I'm bone weary but I can't rest; my adrenaline is too high. Thoughts are running through my mind and my body feels electric. There is so much I want, but I don't know how to get it. Modeling and acting both appeal to me. I'm pretty and slim with a small waist and curvy bottom. I'm taller than most women, and my platinum blonde hair is full and reaches my waist. I can get a foot in the door somewhere in LA. That's where I need to go to make it big. And I will. I know it.

Again the skin on my neck prickles. I shift in my seat and covertly glance behind me. This time he moves, sinks back, pretending to sleep. So he is watching me. Dude, gotcha. I can't help grinning a little. I have that effect on men. Men of all ages. I've had everything from twelve-year-olds to ninety-year-olds ogling me this past year, when I finally bloomed into a woman.

* * *

I jerk when we stop and the driver kills the engine. Rubbing my eyes, I yawn. I must've fallen asleep.

"Thirty minutes," the driver barks.

I stand and stretch, wondering if I can leave my backpack, but decide against it. When I pull it down, I can't help noticing Mr Mysterious's eyes on me again. He's sitting up. I stretch a little extra, showing off my naked midriff, before I smirk, grab my bag and head off the bus.

The older couple is already inside the diner.

The driver looks me over. "Could've left the bag," he mutters.

I breeze past him and enter the greasy place he's chosen for our stop. My stomach growls, but I decide to hold on to my money. A radio is playing 1970s music, and the scent of frying bacon fills the air. I sink into a booth. It's only the five of us here in the middle of the night.

"What'll you have, hon?" A waitress in her fifties, clad in an ill-fitted red dress has snuck up on me.

"Just water, please."

"You've gotta order something."

Crap.

"She'll have milkshake and a burger," says someone with a deep baritone behind me. "And fries. Lots of 'em." I spin around. There stands the mysterious passenger. He looks like he's in his forties, tall, weathered, dirty-blond hair. His body appears tight underneath a tattered leather jacket and blue jeans. Brown eyes, so dark they're nearly black, a nose that looks like it's taken a beating or two. It makes him look dangerous, but in a good way. Like a movie star, an action hero. He's got a bit of a Mickey Rourke vibe, before all the plastic surgery.

"Same for me, hon. And add coffee to that," he says to

the waitress and she trots off, hips swaying. "This seat taken?" He indicates the seat across the table.

"Eh... Of course it isn't. Help yourself."

"Thought maybe you wanted to fraternize with the charming driver."

I scoff and look over to the fat man at the counter, ordering just about everything on the menu.

"You didn't have to order anything for me. I wasn't hungry."

"Oh, please. I know a starving girl when I see her. Indulge me." His knee brushes against mine under the table. The touch of his rough jeans on my naked skin sends off a bolt of excitement through me, making my nipples stiffen. He doesn't miss it, glancing at my breasts and up again. When he meets my eyes, something flickers in them. Something naughty.

Oh please. I know a starving man when I see one.

I let my gaze wander over his broad chest and then back up. Meeting his eyes from under lowered eyelashes, I bite my lip. Starving, and hot as hell.

"I'm Jake." He extends a hand, and when I take it a rush of excitement runs through me.

"Anya."

"Anya... Love the name."

"Crazy mom."

"Not at all, hon. It fits you like a glove. You're" —his gaze travels to my breasts— "all Anya. All the way." When his gaze wanders up again, there's something predatory in his eyes.

I lick my lips and clear my throat that's turned dry.

Two milkshakes, two large plates with hamburgers and

fries, and a coffee arrives. It breaks the moment, for which I'm grateful. I nearly lost my breath there. Our conversation moves on to simpler things for a little while. When he asks about my plans for LA, I get excited again and tell him about my dreams. He says he knows people there. He'll introduce me.

Jake watches me eat. It's as if he's devouring every bite I take. I'm well aware of what he thinks of me, and I bet he's hard as a rock. I'm not usually into older men, but he is really freaking hot, and I want him to like me.

The bus driver announces that we need to hit the road. I need the restroom first.

"Please don't let him leave without me."

"Not a chance... Anya." He winks.

When I get back out, they've boarded, except Jake who meets me with a coffee to go in his hand.

"I figured you'd want one." He shrugs and smiles.

"Oh, it's perfect! Thank you."

It's only natural I join him in the rear of the bus. He keeps asking about me while I sip on the coffee. There's not much to tell. I let him know about the pathetic little life I've lived. Mom. Dad. School. Friends. Cheerleading. Sucky grades.

"Any boyfriend?"

I shake my head.

"Come on, a hot chick like yourself."

I laugh and arch, showing off my ample assets. He all but licks his lips.

"But you're no virgin, are you?"

My eyes grow wide as I stare at him. His gaze is decidedly hungry. He's playing with me. Oh, I know this game, and I love it. I'm not very experienced, but I'm most certainly no virgin.

"No..." I lick my lips and smile.

His thigh brushes mine. I don't mind it. In fact, it sets off a tingling sensation that shoots straight to the pit of my belly. When I don't object, he moves his leg again, and lets his thigh stay pressed against mine. The rough fabric of his jeans scrapes against my bare skin.

"Had many boys, then?" He leans close, his breath hot on my cheek. He smells of sandalwood, outdoorsy. Like a cowboy. Minus cow.

I smile lazily, my heart rate picking up. "Mmno..."

A hand on my naked thigh. Just resting there. "How many, Anya. Tell me. How many went here?" His hand moves up along the inside of my thigh, brushing against the crotch of my jeans shorts.

A bolt of excitement shoots up to my nipples. I swallow hard. "A few..."

"A few, huh?" His fingers press against the hard seam and make tiny circles on the fabric. My eyes nearly roll back in my head from the unexpected touch. He pushes harder, making me jump.

"How many, Anya?" His voice is husky and his fingers move, finding the softness on the inside of my thigh, right where cloth meets skin. They caress back and forth, shooting bolts of heat right to my pussy.

"Two," I moan. "Two." I arch and shudder as his fingers

prod a little deeper, pushing in between the fabric, touching the edge of my panties. I gasp. "Oh God."

"Two, huh? Two fucked this little cunt?" He pushes my panties a little to the side and finds my slick folds. I spread my thighs, glancing around the bus. No one seems to notice anything. He circles around my entrance. The insides of my thighs tingle. His nasty words ignite a burning furnace inside me, but no, this is wrong. I put my hand on his and try to push it away.

He laughs. "S'alright, babe. Relax. I'm gonna take care of you. Come here."

He snakes an arm around my back and his hand finds my nipple, pinching it. I inhale sharply, crying out, and his hand darts up to cover my mouth.

He chuckles in my ear. "Be quiet, little one. Be a good girl and shut up."

His hand stays firmly on my mouth. His other leaves my pussy and finds my breasts. He's rough. It hurts, and is so fucking good at the same time. I moan, and he pulls me to him, the hand covering my mouth nearly crushing my lips. He keeps it there as his other hand wanders south again, over my belly. He flips the belly button piercing then dips inside my shorts, finding his way under my panties.

His groan reverberates through me. "Waxed. Oh, you naughty girl. You're practically begging to be fucked, aren't you? Such a slut." He pushes his hand further, finding my clit, pinching it. I buck up and let out a muffled cry against his hand. He hushes me and removes his hand from my pussy, fiddling, unzipping my shorts. "Your body is fucking heaven, Anya."

With better access he shoves his whole hand down

between my legs in one rough move and pushes his fingers inside me. I arch and moan again. He thrusts his fingers in me. Hard. My mind is spinning. I'm insanely turned on and worried at the same time. Worried that this is wrong.

"Not a sound, or I'll have to punish you. Got it?"

I want to object. I'm no slut, but his hand feels too good and it overrides whatever else my mind is trying to tell me.

He thrusts his fingers deep inside and whispers in my ear. "Nod, and I'll be really good to you."

I want good. Good is nice. I nod.

He removes his hand and lifts me with ease so I half sit on his lap. My head lolls back on his chest. I listen to his heavily thudding heart as he wiggles my shorts past my hips. He keeps mumbling curses. Lots of curses, and lots of dirty words: I'm a slut, a filthy little girl who's gonna get what I deserve.

I need his hand back between my legs. If that makes me a slut, then I'm a slut.

He yanks my shorts past my knees and then off me. A waft of cool air hits my pussy. He moves on the seat, shifts me again and pushes me down, my head in his lap.

"Open your mouth," he growls, his breathing heavy.

I don't understand. He shoves a hand between my legs, thrusting his fingers inside my pussy again. Too hard. I gasp, and as I open my mouth, he pushes his cock inside. I gag, but he grips the back of my head and pushes deep. Deeper than I've ever taken a guy before. I put my hands on his hips and try to back away. I need to breathe, but he has lodged his cock deep in my throat. He keeps it there as one hand again moves to my pussy, circle my clit, push inside. Then he lets me breathe. One breath only, and then it goes deep inside again. I moan as saliva dribbles over my chin.

It makes him groan. He thrusts slowly, in and out. "Oh baby, do that again."

I do it, but only because I try to tell him I need to breathe. It's hell and heaven at the same time. I'm so fucking wet. It's insane. He makes it so good for me between my legs and so fucking uncomfortable in my throat. Finally he slips his cock out of my mouth with a shudder. It's glistening wet with my spit.

"Not yet. I've got all night. I've got so much I'm gonna do with you, my little diamond." He lifts me on top of him, so I'm straddling his thighs, and then he pushes inside me with a groan. My eyes fly open and I cry out. His cock is huge, and he stretches me far more than I've experienced before in my short life. He slams a hand over my mouth again.

"I told you to be quiet. You're asking to be punished."

He grabs my hips and lifts me a little, pumping my pussy, his breathing labored. He rocks back and forth as a hand travels up to my breast, pinching a nipple hard. I moan, which makes him pull out and flip me over on my belly. I feel a finger on my rear entrance, pushing, prodding. He pushes it inside and I jerk, my hands fly up to defend myself, but he grabs both my wrists, and hold them in a firm grip. I'm completely at his mercy.

He leans over me. "Someone go here before? Someone fucked your ass?"

"No." My voice trembles.

He gives out a guttural groan. "Good. Such a good little

virgin ass." He leans heavily on me. "I'm gonna fuck your ass. I'm gonna shove my thick cock all the way in."

My heart rate picks up, and my mouth turns dry even though my whole body tingles with anticipation. "No, I... I mean..."

He pushes fingers inside my pussy and my ass, thrusting, deeper and deeper. My thighs shake and my insides burn as if touched by fire. It's so good.

"Yes, babe. You're gonna take my cock, and you're gonna love it." He holds me down as he moves again. He pushes inside my dripping wet pussy and begins to fuck me really hard. I can't tell up from down. He slams a hand over my mouth and chuckles when I begin to pant louder and louder.

"Shhh. Be a good girl for me."

I nod and bite my lips to stay quiet. I agree with the sentiment. I don't like the thought that the three other people in the bus might notice what we're doing.

He removes his hand from my mouth and pushes a finger inside my ass as he keeps fucking me. It stings. I try to clench against it, but I have no resistance. I'm too caught up in the onslaught of lust. He pulls out. Both finger and cock. I feel something cold and wet between my ass cheeks, then something much thicker than a finger pushes against the little hole. It's not possible. That can't fit! I gasp and squirm. His thrusts are shallow, but he's adding a little depth with each thrust. I want to beg him no. The pressure is unbelievable. A hand snakes around to my front and fingers circle my clit, my thoughts shatter and I nearly cry from the pulsating feeling that grows between my legs. I clench and unclench, but my body isn't offering much resistance, and he keeps gaining depth. It burns. My ass is on fire. He can't possibly go deeper. Oh god, his finger on my clit feels good.

"Such a good girl." He groans. "Soon you're all mine. I'm gonna fuck you all night, babe. It's a long, long ride."

He thrusts, deeper, deeper, with more force. His hand rubs my clit. Tension rises in my body, pools between my legs. My ass burns. Heat spreads in my pussy. I arch and moan, and as I come undone in a series of rapid convulsions, he shoves his cock all the way in. Deep, fucking insanely deep, and thrusts with abandon.

"You like this, you naughty little princess," he pants.

I don't move. I can't move. The force of his thrusts rubs me against the rough fabric of the seats, rubs my tits and burns the sharp angles of my hip bones. My ass feels as if it's tortured in the fires of hell, but it's a good pain at the same time.

"I'm gonna come in your ass. Your tight hole is so good. So fucking good."

He pumps a few more times and then his cock twitches to life as he stills, rooted balls deep in me. Falling on top of me, he caresses my hair, wrapping it around his fist, pulling my head to the side and crashes his mouth against mine. We don't move. His chest is warm and sweaty against my back, and he's breathing hard. Finally, he pulls out, fiddles with something and begins to pull my panties back along my legs. When he's covered me up, he wraps his arms around me and pulls me to him. I settle in his embrace, my limbs shaking. I squirm. I'm still turned on. His strong arms and how they feel against my skin doesn't help relaxing me. He moves his hands exploring my body, when they find my breasts, he squeezes them hard enough to bruise, rolling my nipples between his fingers.

I keen and arch, gritting my teeth against the exquisite pain.

"You're a right little slut, aren't you, Anya?"

"No," I moan.

He pinches harder. "Yes you are. Tell me you are a slut. Tell me you are my slut."

I'm no— Ow!"

He chuckles. "Quiet, little one. Or do you want grandma and grandpa over there to come look? Maybe you'd get off on that? Tell me what you are," he growls in my ear. One hand comes down and dives inside my panties, where his fingers start toying with my clit.

"Oh god."

"What are you?" His fingers move, circle, push, thrust inside. My head spins.

My thighs start shaking, my toes curl and the next orgasm rips through my body. My lips barely obey me. "Slut... I'm your slut. Oh my god!"

He chuckles. "I'm no god, hon. I'm the fucking devil, but I can make you soar. I'll fuck you. Again and again. I'm gonna come in your mouth, in your ass, on your tits. I'll ruin this precious little girl, and you're gonna love every moment." He leans closer, whispering in my ear. "Tell me you'll enjoy me penetrating your every hole." His fingers thrust inside me, almost cruel in their force. "You make me hard again. Fucking hell. Take off your panties. Slowly." He pushes me on my back. "Lift your ass and pull them down, then spread your legs and show me your wet cunt. Your sweet, young pussy."

I hook my thumbs inside the hem of my panties and push them off me, inch by inch, wriggling as if I'm struggling. I don't let go of his gaze, but Jake is having a real hard time deciding where to focus.

"Fuck, you're hot," he growls with a thick voice.

I let my thighs fall apart and put my hand to my pussy, playing with my clit, dipping inside my slit.

"Like what you see?" I ask, my voice sultrier than I've ever heard it before. It's a rush. I love this, having this power over a man. He's mesmerized watching me play with myself. The tip of his thick cock strains to burst free from his underwear.

"Oh hell yes. You're a very naughty girl. I think you have a bright future ahead of you." A wicked grin spreads over his face. He frees his cock in one swift move, falls on top of me and pushes inside. He's so rough I lose my breath. I manage a little whimper. He covers my mouth with one hand as he begins to pound me.

I moan against his hand again, but not because it's uncomfortable. It's really fucking crazy nice. I want more. I want deeper.

"M—ore," I mouth.

"More, huh? You whore. You filthy, wonderful, fuckable little whore." He shoves his cock inside me again, hard, brutal; a hand on my throat, squeezing until I can barely breathe. "If you're really good, I'll let the bus driver have a go at you as well. I bet you'd like that. He looks well-hung, if a bit fat. I'll let him fuck you while I bury my cock deep in your throat."

This should disgust me, but the pure nastiness of what he says makes me explode when I come again. He moves relentlessly in me, then suddenly pulls out and yanks up my shirt and bra in one move. His cum squirts all over my belly and tits, creating hot thick rivers on my skin. His eyes glint as he smears it, pinching my breasts until I want to scream with pain and pleasure alike. He shoves his cum-covered fingers between my lips.

"Lick me clean."

I touch them with the tip of my tongue, tasting his salty juices. He groans and thrusts his fingers in and out in my mouth a few times before he wipes them on my shirt. He moves lower and circles his fingers around my soaked slit, dipping inside, pinching my clit, slapping it, then inside again. His hand switches direction, and he mercilessly pushes his slippery fingers deep in my ass again. I buck a little from the pain.

"You liked that, didn't you? Never say no to me again. I know what's best for you."

The pressure keeps increasing as he adds more fingers, thrusting hard and fast. He circles my clit with his other hand and suddenly it isn't that bad anymore. My stomach clenches. I don't want it, but my body revels in it. My soul blackens with shame, but he feels so fucking good.

"Do you want the driver here, Anya? In your ass?" He leans over me and whispers in my ear. His breath smells of coffee and faintly of whiskey. "Or do you want me there again? The night is long."

I arch, trembling. It's so good.

"Look at me, Anya." His voice is hoarse, a growl that sends a shiver of fright up my spine. "I'm keeping you. We're gonna have a lot of fun together. I'll show you the stars, lay the world at your feet. And you're gonna do everything I ask of you. Every nasty little thing I want you to do."

I shake my head. I think I'm shaking my head. I squeeze my eyes shut. I'm so confused. Yes, I want the stars. Give me the stars. And more of this! But nasty? Whore?

"No... I... " I whimper.

"Oh yes, I am. You're coming with me when I get off this ride." He leans closer. "So easy. So young. So malleable. Next stop, I'll ask the ogling driver to join in. Bet he's frustrated as fuck. Bet he hasn't been inside a woman for years. Bet he's really nasty."

Jake shoves his hand inside me again, wiggling his fingers. My eyes roll back in my head as I arch and moan. I picture the driver pounding my pussy while Jake shoves his cock deep in my throat. The thought makes my belly ache so hard I nearly double over.

"What's the take away-lesson from this, Anya?"

I shake my head. A tear rolls down the side of my cheek, but I don't know if it's because I'm so turned on, or because I'm afraid.

"Don't run away from home."

Part Two

Firefighter's Pet

Smoke billows up from the side of the seven-story-high apartment building. Three windows on the third floor are completely engulfed in flames. Twirling, twisting shapes of orange and yellow – a deadly, ferocious furnace – licks the façade and blackens it. The heat bends the metal on the windowsills.

I push through the crowd, widening my eyes in excitement. "Hey, what happened?" I ask the nearest bystander, nudging him with my elbow.

The wrinkly old man next to me shrugs and spits out a toothpick. "Dunno. That's one *miiighty* fire, though."

"Yeah! It sure is." My heart pounds as I take in the incredible sight before me. The fire is a living, breathing thing. Beautiful and terrifying.

A loud shatter from a window breaking makes me flinch. I gape in awe, watching as a ladder from a fire engine rises to a balcony one floor above the fire. A woman stands in the plume of smoke. She screams in anguish for someone to help her, a primal sound that runs a shiver down my back. My heart speeds up even further. I inch closer and closer to the plastic tape sealing off the yard and look around me, taking in the surreal vision. The whole place is full of fire trucks, hoses, puddles of water, and men. Lots and lots of men.

Is it a stupid cliché to say firemen are hot? Well, yes, but they *are*. Really fucking, crazy hot. One man in particular caught my attention the moment he exited the building, pulling off a gas mask, his helmet and a hood. He is sooty, tall and broad chested and wears the equipment like a warrior, as if it has been tailored with him in mind. I almost drool as I take in his strong jawline, hay-colored hair, and defined cheekbones. He climbed the ladder while it rose, a mission that looked beyond insane, screaming danger, and now he wraps his massive arm around the waist of the woman and clutches her to his chest. It all happens so fast. There's the flames and the smoke, hoses sneaking across the front yard, and water shooting into the fire, men shouting. They're so *efficient* and organized despite the chaos. Me, I'm a mess any day, and with a disaster like this... I don't function at all.

A shudder runs through me. *Man*, I want to be her. I want those arms around *me*: muscles of steel, crushing me to him. Heat runs through me, scorching me like the fire before me, pulsating between my legs. If I could just...

It's not like I think it through. I'm not one to ponder things in excess. I'm a girl who acts. After looking left and right to make sure no one's paying attention to me, I slide toward the foliage at the far side. Sidling through the other gawking bystanders, I take aim for bushes that will cover me. I can't be seen, or I'm screwed.

Fires make an insane noise. The roar devours all other sounds, deafening me with its ferocity. I haven't been running, but I'm still out of breath when I reach the back of the house where there are no people and no flames. Smoke seeps out from a half-open window a couple of floors above me. I'm not sure what I'm doing, but I... Aaaaand bingo. Back door. It even stands ajar.

Inside, the stench of smoke is insane. It's much more intense than I expected. The fire *is* like three floors up, after all. Coughing, I pull up my blouse to cover my mouth and nose, and my eyes tear up immediately. Voices from the front of the house make me press against the wall, hiding behind the staircase, next to a couple of bikes and an old pram. I peek out to see if it's *my* man, but it's some other guys. Hot too, but not *him*. When the sounds of people fade, I sneak around the corner and dash up the first flight of stairs. My hands feel oily and dirty, and when I glance at them, they're black with soot. Oh, that's perfect. I wipe my grimy palms over my face, then crouch and wait. He's bound to come back inside again, right? If he doesn't, this will be such a major fail and damn embarrassing. I don't want any old firefighter to rescue me. I want the man with the golden hair

Adrenaline courses through me when I hear voices again. A glance through the bars of the railing, and my heart jumps up to my throat. Thank you, Lord! Mr. Tall, Blond, and Handsome is on his way up the stairs, pulling a hose.

I time it perfectly, and I *should* get points for the added dramatics. When he sets his boot on the landing where I sit, I dart forward and fall right before him, whimpering, coughing.

"*Help*," I wheeze. "Help. I can't—" I clutch my throat and gag. "The smoke and... Fire... I don't want to *die*."

Tears well up in my eyes as I scramble forward and grab his gloved hand. Actually, the tears are real. The smoke stings like fuck and the air I breathe seems toxic. It's terrifying. I definitely need to get out of here. In the back of my head something says *stupid-stupid-stupid* with increasing urgency. What the hell am I thinking?

"Hey!" he yells. "We got another one." He scoops me up in his arms and holds me to his chest as he turns and hurries down the stairs, toward the front door. "Don't worry. You're safe now. Can you walk on your own?"

Tingles erupt everywhere his massive arms hold me. Hey... maybe stupid, but... can someone say *reward*?

I shake my head and snuggle closer to his chest. He reeks of smoke and danger, feels eternally safe, and carries me as if I weigh nothing. I'm a big girl. No man has ever made me feel small and vulnerable. Not until now. Throwing my arms around his neck, I sigh and push up my chest. When you've got something to flaunt, you flaunt it. Mercilessly.

"You saved my life," I breathe. "What's your name?" My mouth is dry, and my chest feels a little too tight. It was scarier than I'd planned for it to be, sitting in that smoke-filled stairwell.

Amazingly blue eyes peer down at me, flicker to my chest and then back. I bite my lower lip and throw him my naughtiest gaze, hoping he'll catch on, hoping he'll see *me*.

"Mike," he says in a clipped tone, giving me an odd look as he puts me down next to a waiting ambulance, then he turns to the two paramedics. "Might've inhaled some smoke—"

I cough to counter that measly 'might'. Yeah, *duh*! Lots, and lots of goddamn smoke. I needed rescue like no other. I get an oxygen mask snapped on my face as Mike turns and shouts to his colleagues that he's going back in. I want to say something to make him stay with me, but freeze when he speaks again, addressing another firefighter next to him.

"I could have sworn we'd gotten all of them out. Where the fuck did *she* come from?"

The paramedics talk, poke and prod, I answer them, but I don't know what we're saying. *Crap.* My cheeks grow hot, and my stomach sinks with the feeling of having done something really bad. I pull off the mask, hop off the gurney then take off down the street, ignoring the shouts behind me.

* * *

Shame sears through me, and the agony over what I have done is real. I risked my life. I risked someone else's life. For what? For a moment of being the damsel in distress? How incredibly stupid. And still I'm hot and bothered, wondering how I could get hold of this man. I want to feel his strong arms around me again, feel weightless as he lifts me, crushes me against a wall and fucks me silly.

Work in retail is rough.

Work in retail when you get no sleep because you're horny as all hell is a nightmare. I'm not in the mood for customer service.

On the third night after the fire, as I'm brushing my

teeth, two knocks sound on the door, followed by three lighter raps that have me jumping in surprise. I spit out the foam and quickly rinse my mouth before I make my way to the door, pulling on a short robe to cover up my tiny pajamas. There's no hiding the big fluffy white slippers with a cute bunny head, though. Three more impatient knocks make me jerk. After I hook the safety chain in place, I open the door a sliver.

"Yeah?"

Boots. Legs, long strong legs. A large hand fisted around the base of a bouquet of tall red roses. My heart shoots to my throat. *What?* Then the bouquet is lowered and the man behind it reveals himself. Bright blue eyes, a squared jaw. Mischief written all over his face.

"Good evening, miss."

I gasp.

Gods, have mercy on a poor single woman's heart!

"Mike! Hi... wow. How did you find me?"

"You left your name with the paramedics, and in a town of this size... Wasn't too hard. You *wanted* me to find you, didn't you?"

His smile is full of sinful promises of everything I've hoped for, every naughty dream I've ever had. His gaze travels lower, over my breasts, stopping there a moment, making me feel as if he's physically touching them, before he takes in the rest of me. I'm painfully aware of my too-cute slippers that don't match the rest of my much sexier outfit and decide that distraction is the best course of action. I drop my hand and let the gap in the front of the robe widen. My nipples tighten from his inspection, and it clearly doesn't pass him unnoticed. I swallow hard as I take him in. Cowboy boots, black jeans, black T-shirt and an equally black leather jacket. All hard planes and oozing of sex.

Epic.

"Are you gonna let me in?" His voice is a husky baritone that reverberates right through me.

I shouldn't. I shouldn't. It's stupid. Like... I really shouldn't! *Quiet, inner sane voice!* I smooth out an invisible wrinkle on the front of my pajama shorts. A slight shiver of excitement courses through me, then I cock my head and meet his gaze with a side smile.

Oh. My. Fucking. God. I'm doing this.

Chain unhooked, I let the door swing open.

"I'm... not dressed." I throw him a coy glance.

Mike pushes the door closed behind him and drops the flowers on the little side table, moving closer, towering over me. "I think you're just enough dressed."

"For what?" I take a step back as he advances on me.

"For me, Veronica Sanchez." He pulls at the strap of my top, lets it snap back into place, then moves in on me, forcing me against the wall. "You've been a really, really naughty girl, haven't you?"

My heart speeds up, and I swallow hard. He stands so close I can feel the heat of his chest against my breasts. If he moves even the slightest bit closer, we will touch. *Oh, what the hell.* Closing the distance between us, I press up against him, my soft curves meeting his hard planes. The victory is undeniable and immediate. His indrawn breath is sharp as he looks down on me, his gaze falling to my best assets. Then he grins.

"Is it this you want?" I raise an eyebrow.

The look in his eyes is definitely appreciative, but there is also a hint of something darker that makes my stomach clench and my need even more intense. I picked out the right dirty firefighter for sure. Mike possesses secrets, and I'm gonna get to unravel them before tonight is over.

"Mm-hmm. Daddy wants this, and much, *much* more." He moves forward, presses me against the wall and pushes my arms up above my head. My wrists clasped in one of his hands, he strokes my cheek, along the side of my neck, past my collarbone and down to a nipple which immediately turns into a hard peak. He pinches it and leans in, his cheek to mine, his lips brushing my earlobe.

Daddy! For all that is holy, I homed in on the right big bad man.

"I want your body, your soul, and your utter and complete obedience, little Veronica."

My name rolls off his tongue, hot and smooth like melted chocolate and filled with dark promises, the sound almost making me double over. I close my eyes and inhale his rich scent of fresh wood and moss, outdoorsy, like the wind and the sun.

"Look at me, girl."

His stern voice makes my nethers quiver. I obey in an instant and snap open my eyes to meet his glacial gaze.

"Turn around. Palms flat on the wall. Spread your legs."

My heart almost jumps out of my chest, and a wave of heat hits my pussy. "Yes, Daddy," I whisper.

His eyes glint with an untamed, raw lust that makes me want to fall to my knees and pray for him to touch me and take me. When he lets go of my hands, I spin around, a syrupy feeling settling between my legs.

"Aren't you a sight, babe."

Warm, strong hands slide around my waist, moving up to cup my breasts. The groan that escapes him rumbles through me as he presses his chest to my back. He pinches my nipples through the fabric of my top, rolls the hard peaks between his fingers, and pinches again, harder. I moan and arch into him. This is everything. Forbidden. Exciting. The fire. The stupid act I pulled. All worth it. *So* worth it.

"Let's get this off you." He pulls my top over my head in one swift move, leaving goose bumps chasing each other along my arms.

I let out a new moan. "I want to feel you," I whisper. Shivers run through me as he drags his fingers along my side, down to my hip.

"Shhh. There'll be plenty of time for that. Keep your hands against the wall, baby." He hooks a finger inside the waistband of my shorts then slides his finger between the fabric and my skin, setting me alight. "Do you want me to free you of these?"

I look over my shoulder, measuring him through a curtain of my thick black curls. "Are you asking?" I release a little nervous-sounding giggle, then snap my mouth shut as tension rises between us. A slight tremor runs through me. He doesn't come off as the asking type of guy, but rather the type who takes what he wants, and I happen to be exactly what he wants tonight.

He laughs. "Not really."

The deep, sexy rumble that is his voice makes me want

to ignore any and all commands about keeping my hands on the wall and instead turn around and rip off his clothes, but I fight my impulses. I'm *so* in for this ride. He pulls down the shorts slowly, inch by inch, teasing them off me. The fabric sliding over my skin, and the promises of pleasure it brings, makes me short of breath. I squirm and am immediately rewarded with a slap on my ass. It's not hard, but it comes unexpectedly and makes me squeal.

"Hey!"

He chuckles as he drops the shorts to the floor then drags a large, warm palm up along the inside of my leg, closer and closer to an increasingly aching part *right* where my thighs meet. A finger brushes past my swollen nether lips through the fabric of my panties, making my insides quiver, then he grabs my hips and twists me around.

"On your knees! Let that pouty mouth of yours do some real work instead of spouting big little lies."

My cheeks heat up. Busted. So fucking busted. When I hesitate, he grabs my chin and tilts up my head. His blue eyes catch my full attention, so cold, and so *hot* at the same time. Like the cloudless sky on one of those heated August afternoons, when the asphalt melts and the world becomes unbearable for a few hours until the sun goes down and the night cools the land. He's *that* intense. My mind has a massive meltdown, and it's a long, long time until sunset.

"I'm not here to drink tea and get to know you, babe. I smelled it all over you, how you wanted me."

Mm-hmm, fuck yes!

"Well, here I am. You don't know me—"

Well, not yet.

"—I sure don't know you, but you look like a girl who

knows how to have some fun, and I'm all for fun and games. So, get on your knees and take out my cock. I want to see you wrap those lush lips around it as I pound your throat."

He grabs my nape, takes a firm hold of my hair and pushes me down. My pussy floods with heat as I sink down, and my bared nipples turn into hard nubs, tingling with arousal. I kneel before his two strong, jeans-clad legs, flatten my palms on his thighs and caress my way up to his belt, very purposely brushing past the hard bulge that has me salivating. Belt unbuckled, I undo the top button and pull down the zipper, one tooth at a time. His grip in my hair tightens.

"You tease," he growls.

I hide the grin. *Oh yes.* He's not the only one who can play games. Heat, and a clean, musky scent reaches my nostrils when I push apart the zipper and caress the rock-hard shape under the fabric of his briefs.

"Girl," he gasps, "get on with it."

Fingers hooked inside the waistband of his briefs, I pull them down until his erect cock springs free. De-*fucking-*licious! The size of it nearly makes me double over with want.

"Take me in your mouth."

I glance up at the man before me, his eyes half closed, his teeth digging into his lower lip. Raising my eyebrows, I wrap my fingers around the base of his cock and swirl my tongue over the silky head. His groan of pleasure is my reward when I take him in my mouth.

"Hands behind your back." His tone is firm, leaving no room for objections.

I obey immediately, eager to please this Viking, this blond firefighter-angel, and clasp one wrist in the other hand. Mike takes a firmer grip of my hair, pushes deeper and hits the back of my throat, making me gag. I push at his thighs in an instinctive response, forgetting all about his demand.

"Ah-ah. You have a really hard time following orders, don't you?"

I guiltily hide my hands again as he pulls back a little and gives me a small reprieve.

"You're so pretty with my cock buried in your face, girl. You should never do anything else with that mouth. Touch yourself. Put a hand inside your panties and look at me the whole time."

I don't have to be told twice. My pussy is soaked as I slide a finger along my swollen, slick folds, twitching when I pass my clit. Circling it again and again, I find a rhythm that sets my insides aflame. Lucky I have the perfect man for the job right before me. I'm in *dire* need of saving from this furnace.

"Oh god," I groan, but with his cock buried deep in my throat, it comes out as an incoherent mumbling.

He shudders and grips my hair tighter as he thrusts his hips. "Oh baby, do that again. Make those noises again."

Pushing my fingers inside my pussy, I relax the back of my throat and hum, as he pushes deeper, pulls back, thrusts forward again, groaning so loud it nearly tips me over the edge. Saliva drips on my chest, my scalp aches, and my pussy quivers. I rub my clit faster and harder as he increases his pace, pushing scary deep, deeper than I've ever managed before. Suddenly he pulls out and grabs my neck.

"Get up."

I drool, strands of saliva hanging between my lips and his glistening purple cock, and stand on shaky legs. The back of my throat is sore, pummeled, but the discomfort sends waves of want through me for this gorgeous man to fill another place. I squirm and clench my thighs, pulsating with need, shamefully used, yet desperate for more. His gaze darts down to where my hand is buried in my panties, then he crashes his mouth against mine, pushes his tongue past my lips, and robs me of my breath and every remnant of sanity. He tastes unfamiliar, minty, hot. Cupping my breasts, he pays both thorough attention, squeezing and pinching my nipples until the pain overtakes the pleasure and I try to push him off me. He chuckles and grabs my hands, holding them as he leans in and instead teases my nipples with his teeth and lips, sucking, nipping. The torture is exquisite, and when he pushes one hand inside my panties and finds my soaked pussy, a shock of lust runs through me. I whimper and buck as he thrusts several fingers past my slick entrance.

"So wet for me?" He pushes deeper and wiggles his fingers. "Tell me, Veronica, did it make you hot to break into a burning building and risk the lives of firefighters?"

My heart leaps to my throat. "I didn't— No, I—" I sputter and then I cry out as he stabs his fingers inside me, thrusting hard, in and out. "I'm gonna come," I squeal.

"No, you're not."

"I can't—"

He pulls out his fingers, grabs my shoulders and steers me through the corridor toward my bedroom at the far end, towering over me as he backs me up against the bed. I jerk when my calves hit the bed frame. He narrows his eyes as he studies my face before his gaze drops to my chest.

"Turn around and bend forward." His voice is stern, and the icy sharpness makes my heart jolt.

"W—what are you doing?"

"Now."

I swallow hard and turn. I have a bad feeling about this. Bad as fuck, and still I want whatever he'll dish out and more.

He puts a large palm on my lower back and pushes forward. "Bend over. Now. Hands flat on the mattress."

A shiver races through me as I slowly heed his command. My heart pounds like crazy. I've never in my life felt so vulnerable as I do in this moment, unable to look at him, my ass up in the air. And still... I've never felt so alive, so in the *now*.

I put my palms against the cool soft sheet, a vague scent of my green apple fabric softener reaching my nostrils from the newly laundered fabric.

"Sink lower. Push up your ass."

My breath hitches as I slide further forward, my upper body moulding against the mattress. I yelp when he forces my feet apart with a rough push of his knee between my thighs.

"Good girl. Now don't move. Not one inch."

"What are you going to do?" My voice is husky, tainted with tension and a little dose of apprehension.

"You've been a bad, bad girl."

"No, I—" His hand descends on my butt, the force of the slap sending a shockwave through me. I cry out and try to crawl away, my skin tingling.

He's not having it.

"Did I say you could move? You just earned two more." He holds a hand firm over my back as two more smacks land on the same tender ass cheek.

A wave of heat floods my pussy, as if seeping in from my stinging skin. I moan and squirm, swallowing hard. *Oh my fucking god.* I jolt when his hand touches me, but this time he's tender, stroking over the aching area, and over to the non-hurting half.

"You look so fucking fine, babe." He slides his finger along the side of my panties, then under the fabric. "And you're such a bad girl."

I gasp when he strokes my slick folds, up and down, to my clit, past my entrance, clit again. I arch and whimper, pleading silently that he'll take me.

I try to push against his prodding fingers, but to no avail. A light touch of his lips on my warm butt cheek sends goosebumps racing across my thighs. *Oh, yes, Daddy! Come on!* I tense as his teeth scrape my sensitive skin, and when he bites me at the same time as he thrusts his fingers inside my aching pussy, I cry out loud, almost losing control of my limbs as he moves in me, slowly pushing in and out.

"Deeper," I groan. "Faster."

A hard smack lands on my butt. "Silence. You're not calling the shots here." He pushes more fingers inside me, stretching me deliciously. "You liked that, didn't you?"

Oh fuck yes, I do. I'm embarrassingly wet and blush at the squelching noises his thrusting in my pussy produces. When he pulls out. I clench my fists and groan.

"Palms flat on the bed. Same position. That's four more. If you disobey me again, I'll double it every time."

I immediately flatten my hands then grip the sheet as I prepare for the smacks. My pussy swells at the mere thought. His hand falls on my left cheek once, twice, a third time, a fourth time in quick succession, the force knocking the breath out of me. He rests his hand on my searing skin, stroking it, but I'm so high on the pain, I barely feel it. Then four more rapid smacks follow on the other butt cheek. I have no air in my lungs to even cry out.

"*Why*?" I finally wail. "You already—"

He tsks. "Where are your hands?"

I shudder and glance at my tightly clenched fists. *Oh hell.* It's an overwhelming effort to straighten them, but I do it.

His chest is hot against my back as he leans over me, whispering in my ear. "Did you count?"

"Isn't there supposed to be a safeword for this?" I whimper.

He laughs. "There is. 'I confess.' That is your safeword. You say them, then you call the cops and tell them what a bad girl you've been. Now, did you count?"

My mind is a mess as I try to grasp what he's saying. 'I confess.' Fuck no. I'd rather take the punishment. He strokes my searing skin, and his fingers sweep past my swollen labia, teasingly slow, the fabric of my panties soaked. Four, I realize. And then four. He said he'd double it. *Fuck.*

"Four more?" My voice is ridiculously small. I sound like a little girl who knows she's been bad and is just about to confess to Daddy.

He straightens and delivers two more on each side. I cry out, tears of pain welling up in my eyes. At the same time,

I'm so fucking turned on I can barely breathe. I want to feel him in me so much it hurts. My skin burns beyond belief. I flinch from apprehension when he caresses my ass, but when he drags his fingers past my pussy, I groan with need and bury my face in the mattress.

Yesthankyoulord, are my near-incoherent thoughts as he pulls down my panties, slowly uncovering me, inch by inch. The fabric slides over burning hot flesh. Silky and cool, they tickle my upper thighs as he pulls them lower before he lets them fall to my feet.

He groans and cups my ass in his large palms, grabbing me with rough hands and making it sting even more before he spreads me wide open. Something soft and warm, sweeps over my wet folds. I moan loudly when I realize it's his mouth on me, his tongue pushing inside, then moving to flip over my clit, sucking it, teasing it between his teeth. *Ohmygod!* I shake, unable to remain standing any longer. A sharp pinch on my clit makes me squeal.

"Did I tell you to move?"

"Please don't spank me again!" I blurt out, breathless, my mind spinning.

"Is that a confession I hear coming up?" His voice is a low rumble, maddeningly sexy, with the perfect hint of a threat in it.

"*Mmmno*," I mewl.

"Then how many times?"

I almost panic. How many times? Many. I have no idea. "I don't know. I can't count," I whimper.

"Sixteen," he says, his voice so thick with arousal it makes my stomach clench.

My pussy quivers at the mere thought. I close my eyes and try to control my erratic breathing.

"Keep your eyes closed, and don't move. You *are* allowed to scream."

I gasp for air before he even begins. The anticipation is killing me. Two shockingly strong blows strike my right cheek. I groan but manage to stay where I am. Two more follow on the left cheek, making me lose my breath. I push my flattened palms down hard on the bed, trembling, my pussy vibrating from the heat that shoots from my aching ass. He caresses my skin, slowly, his hands hot and tender, then smacks down four more times on the right side and four more on the left, all of them just about touching my swollen folds. I lose count, feeling as if I'm going to die. My legs shake, but I don't dare move even the slightest. The next would be thirty-two. I can't *do* thirty-two. I'll scream 'I confess' long before he's done.

"Confession time?" He leans over me, his breath fanning my ear, his palm hot on my searing skin.

"Can I shake my head?" I grit out.

"Yes, you may."

I shake my head.

He's quiet. Nothing happens. Then four quick smacks right over my pussy. I scream at the same time as the heat and the pain makes my inner muscles convulse.

"God!" I cry, almost blacking out as I explode in the most intense orgasm I've ever experienced.

As if from a distance, I hear the faint rustling of plastic ripped apart and then he pushes his thick cock inside me all the way in one hard thrust. I cry out again, hoarsely, not even recognizing my own voice. He pulls out almost all the way, then slams inside, rocking me back and forth. I can barely stand, and he grabs my hips, rough fingers digging in bruisingly hard, holding me firmly as he fucks me with abandon. His ruthless pounding sets off yet another orgasm while he simultaneously groans and falls over me with a shudder. I collapse on the bed with him on top, covering every part of my skin as he cradles me.

"You did *so* good," he purrs in my ear. "Good girl."

"It hurts," I whimper.

"Of course."

"You're insane."

"You had it coming, sweetheart."

Yeah, I guess I had. I have been a very, very naughty girl indeed.

Mike pushes up off the bed and in the next moment I hear the zipper. I spin around and reach for the sheet to cover up, suddenly feeling absurdly naked. He strikes immediately by pulling the fabric from my hands.

"Your body is incredible. So fucking sexy. Don't hide it."

"Will I see you again?"

He scoffs. "Why would I want to see you again?"

My mouth falls open as my heart plummets with disappointment. "Oh." *That* was a slap I hadn't anticipated, and it stings a hell of a lot more than the skin on my ass does.

A hand on my cheek, his thumb stroking. I lean in, like a cat petted by her master. I want more. I need more.

"I could have liked you, Veronica, but I like honest, decent people."

I feel like crying and I'm unable to stop my lip from quivering. "I can be good," I whisper. "I can be decent."

When he doesn't answer, I look up, meeting his intensely blue eyes. He cocks his head, something wicked entering his gaze, something that sets off a sucking sensation in my belly.

"How *good* do you plan on being, little one?"

My throat is suddenly parched, and my nipples tighten in anticipation. "I'll do everything to make amends."

"Everything?" He raises an eyebrow.

I nod.

"You know, I wasn't the only one you put in danger with that stunt of yours. You have a lot of making up to do."

My stomach tightens, and a thrill runs through me as I picture myself naked on a mountain of hoses, pushed up against a fire engine, the scent of smoke in my nostrils, and a whole line of strong, able-bodied men waiting to take me and punish me for my bad behavior.

"I'm ready for my punishment... Daddy."

Mike pulls up the corners of his mouth into a wide smile, looking less stern, but no less intimidating. "Good girl," he says and cups my cheek. "My good little pet. So much fire in you."

"Thank God I've found myself a firefighter, then," I say.

Part Three

Demon Lust

A Massage Parlor Naughty Read

It's the hottest day of the summer.

The concrete pavement radiates the heat back at me, and my flip-flops barely protect my feet. The people around me mill about in tiny shorts and barely-there tops, a sheen of perspiration covering tanned skin.

My back aches, and I tilt my head from side to side, wincing as I hear the cracks. I'm in such bad shape.

Everybody else went to the beach while I worked my ass off at the office, finishing my latest project. My asshole of a boss hasn't let me out for weeks, and I have a mountain of overtime piled up. I don't know if I'll ever get any pay for those hours, but I'm climbing my way up in the company, slowly but surely, and in the end it *should* be worth it.

I got a tiny raise a few months back, and a pat on my shoulder. That's... something, I guess.

I *hope* it will be worth it, at least.

Hours by the desk haven't been kind to my body,

though, and I've finally found the time to go get a massage. A friend and co-worker recommended Hans at Taboo Massage Parlor and Tattoos.

Not sure about the name, to be honest, kind of... odd. And what's with the tattoos combined with massage? But she vouched for the best hands she'd ever had on her body and that she'd never been so relaxed after.

I *need* that.

I stop at the sidewalk. The heat makes the air shimmer. The house in front of me is an old red brick building with high, arched windows. As far as I can see, every window is covered with a white curtain. It looks clean, proper, and a little bit ominous.

I wipe the sweat off my neck then push the heavy wooden door open.

A bell tolls once.

When the door falls closed behind me, I'm wrapped in absolute silence, the street sounds gone.

I've entered directly into a waiting room where it's blessedly cool. Every piece of furniture is white, including the carpet. On one wall is a poster with intricate tribal patterns in the shape of a dragon. Black on white. I take a step closer and tilt my head.

No, not a dragon.

It's a snake.

That's the only decoration. I'm about to look away when something moves in the pattern. I look again, but it's just a painting. Weird. Maybe I have a heat stroke?

"Hello?"

No answer. I chew on my lip.

There's one door. Do I open it? Or will I walk directly

into a massage session and embarrass everyone? I'm unsure of what to do, but I'm ten minutes early, so I decide to sit and wait.

There's a small note on the door. I walk up to it and squint as I read.

'Turn off your cell phone. Sit. Close your eyes. Wait.'

I look around me, then I shrug and sink into the couch. Hesitating, I then obey and turn off my phone.

All right. Did as you asked. What now?

Such a weird place.

I drum my fingers on my naked thigh, pull down my short skirt a little, and look around me.

'Close your eyes.'

All right. Fine.

In the dark, my senses sharpen, and my breaths, my heartbeat, and the sensation of fabric on slick skin becomes enhanced, almost overwhelming.

I wait.

I wonder if I'm being watched.

* * *

"Miss Carmichael."

I fly up off the couch, my heart in my throat, dizzy and disoriented. "Yes! Here!"

Oh baby! *Hot!*

Hans, I assume, dressed in loose white cotton pants and a white shirt, sleeves rolled up, his muscular arms covered in tattoos. White-blond thick, unruly hair and piercing blue eyes.

I close my mouth and wipe my chin, just to be sure I haven't drooled.

A smile pulls at the corner of his mouth, and he gestures at the open door behind him. "You are welcome to enter the inner chamber."

"I'm... I'm here for a massage...?"

My hormones have jumped to life all of a sudden, and I struggle to remember actual English words.

"Of course. That is what I do. Welcome. I'm Hans," he purrs with a hint of a foreign accent, maybe German.

His gaze follows me as I pass him, and tension rises, electricity crackling in the air between us.

I take a few steps into a room that's as white as the waiting room. There's a heady aroma of incense, and barely audible music from a hidden loudspeaker.

The door falls close behind me, and I startle thanks to the sudden sound, a little jittery.

It's as if I've entered another world.

In the middle of the room stands a massage table, there's a shelf with a few books, some neatly folded and piled towels, and three lit candles on one wall.

"I will leave you alone for a few minutes while you undress." He hands me a towel. "You can hang your clothes over there and lie down on the table. And relax."

I watch his broad back retreat behind a curtain next to the bookshelf, then I make quick work, following his orders.

After hanging my clothes on a clothes rack, I hop up on the table, lie on my belly, tuck the towel around me, and wait.

And wait.

My senses are hyperaware. I'd hear a needle drop. Or so I think. I nearly jump off the table when a soft male voice speaks over my head.

"I believe you are sufficiently rested. I will move down the towel to your waist."

My heart beats wildly. Where the hell did he come from? How can anyone sneak that silently?

Featherlight fingers bare my shoulders and my upper back. A tiny squirting sound, slick palms rubbing together. I lift my head and look up at him.

"Ah-ah. Close your eyes and relax."

"But... don't you want me to tell you where I hurt and—"

"My fingers will know what you need. Be a good girl now, and close your eyes. Don't open them again until I say so."

I swallow hard, squeeze my eyes shut, and fall back down, resting against the circular pillow with an opening for the face.

Large warm palms descend on my shoulders, moving up and down along my upper spine, straight at first, then up to the sides of my neck.

At first the touch is discreet, barely there, soothing, but soon his fingers dig a little deeper into aching muscles. The slight pain makes me groan. He hushes me.

"You are very tense," he says softly. "Meet the pain, take it in, don't make noises. Remember to breathe. In through your nose, out through your mouth."

I start huffing and puffing.

"Without making noises, Miss Carmichael," he says sternly.

I swallow hard at the demanding tone but do what he says, grinding my teeth against the increasing pain as he works my muscles.

I jerk when he speaks in my ear. "Relax your jaw."

How does he know?

His fingers move to my cheeks, rubbing light circles over the sides. I force my teeth apart and focus on breathing.

"Good girl," he purrs.

He returns to my back. Straight again, then outward, a little more with every stroke.

I gasp when his fingers brush the sides of my breasts. His hands hover there for a second before he continues.

A thrill runs through me, straight to my pussy, and I'm happy I'm lying prone so my nipples don't show, because they've turned into instant hard peaks.

I tense when he pulls the towel a little further south and then resumes the pattern, longer strokes now, deeper. His fingers are like steel rods, digging into my tense body.

"*Breathe*, Miss Carmichael."

"June," I groan.

"I prefer not to get too personal with my customers, Miss Carmichael."

His hands push along my sides, all the way up to my armpits, definitely caressing the soft sides of my breasts.

My breath hitches, then I force myself to follow his orders.

Not personal?

I swallow hard. I think he's getting *very* personal.

His hands perform miracles, and I finally relax as weeks of mounted tension begin to drain out of me. On a downstroke he starts pulling the towel up, covering my back. When I feel cool air on my ass, he snickers.

"Miss Carmichael, I told you to undress."

My heart makes a leap in my chest. He can't mean... "But I thought..." I begin to turn to look at him, but a hand between my shoulders holds me down.

"Don't move. No speaking. Eyes closed. Focus on your breathing, and let me do my job. I shall remove these."

He hooks his fingers inside the waistband of my thong and pulls them downward, uncovering my ass. He drags them along my thighs, past my knees and finally my feet.

My heart beats wildly, and I'm having a really hard time breathing. I'm definitely not relaxing anymore.

I'm naked with a stranger. A stranger who just pulled off my panties.

A squirting noise again, slick palms rubbing against each other, then large warm hands on my butt cheeks.

I try desperately to cling on to the thought that he's a professional, that this is normal. Probably. My friend went here.

Oh *god*, that is nice!

He works my ass the same way he worked my back. First barely-there circling, then deeper, heavier strokes. Fingers pushing into muscles that are so tense the pain brings tears to my eyes. On every outstroke he parts my ass cheeks.

He's gotta see... everything down there.

My cheeks flush with confusing feelings of embarrassment and excitement. Not that I have anything to be excited about. This is just a massage.

A very... thorough and... deeply intimate massage.

Maybe it's a European thing?

Every time he moves back in, I find myself wishing he'd push his fingers just a little bit further. Closer to my center. Because... I have needs.

The thought that he sees me is oddly enticing.

But no.

He grabs the towel again and pulls it down over my butt. I realize I'm grinding my teeth hard and force myself to follow his instructions.

Relax, relax.

But how? God, it's hot in here.

Squirting. More oil.

He grabs my legs and moves them apart a few inches.

My breath gets stuck in my throat, and I twist to look at what he's doing, then I groan and bury my face in the pillow when he starts working my right calf. His thumbs dig deep into my flesh. Pain. Good pain.

Breathe.

His warm hands move up again, past my knee, along my thigh, one hand on the outside and one hand sliding along the inside. His fingers aim straight at my desperate pussy, but stop millimeters away, right before they get there.

I squirm. A heavy, syrupy feeling settles between my legs.

Please, *please*, slip next time. Just a little further.

Calf, knee, thigh. I tremble. And then... stopping right before they reach where I've begun to ache.

I don't have to touch myself to know I'm soaking wet.

He's a pro. He's a pro.

I repeat it as a mantra.

My other leg gets the same attention.

My head spins, and I arch when he almost, *almost*

reaches my pussy. Suddenly there's a heavy weight on my butt and a hand gripping my neck.

"Do not move, Miss Carmichael, or I will need to punish you."

I gasp.

"What?" I try to move, to get up, but his hand on my neck keeps me firmly in place. He's what, like twice my size, probably more. I haven't got a chance.

His breath is on my ear. "Do you want me to continue the treatment?" Voice husky, a soft purr, sending shivers down my spine.

I should say 'hell no', but I can't. I *need* to be here. I need more.

I nod, my movement so restricted that it probably doesn't show. "Yes."

"Yes what?"

"...yes, please?"

"What do you want me to do?"

My breaths stutter pitifully as I whisper, "Continue the treatment."

His hand disappears. "Good girl. Remember the rules."

I nod again, squeeze my eyes shut, and try desperately to focus on my breathing.

Hans resumes massaging my legs, this time both legs at the same time, heavy strokes upward along the outsides of my thighs, then along the insides, almost all the way.

Up, inside.

A touch.

A tiny brush on my pussy lips.

Did I imagine it?

My heart goes crazy, slamming against my ribcage.

I hold my breath as his hands move up again, his thumbs brushing my folds, barely, but they *do*. This time, they really do. He separates my ass cheeks as his kneading brings him all the way up to my lower back.

I ache. A new kind of ache. I must be leaving a wet spot on his pristine sheet.

Moving back down again, he focuses on my thighs, his thumbs stroking along the sensitive insides, all the way up.

A light pressure against my soaked folds before it disappears. With every upward stroke, he touches me.

There.

When the pads of his thumbs suddenly continue upward, along my slick core, up along the inside of my ass cheeks, I can't help the moan, despite his order that I stay silent. His palms continue under the towel, all the way along my back, up to my neck, where he stops as the nape.

He lifts the towel off me.

"Turn around, Miss Carmichael. Lie on your back."

I lick my lips, then swallow hard. As I turn, I'm acutely aware of my naked state.

I glance at him. I don't know what I expected, but he stands coolly, towel in hand, patiently waiting for me to finish the turn.

He adjusts the head rest and places the towel so it covers my hips and my flaming red bush.

I'm almost disappointed.

"Rules," he says sternly.

I immediately close my eyes.

He starts massaging my pecs, below my collarbone, outward to my shoulders. Soft at first, then firmer.

I twitch from the pain, then remember to internalize it like he said.

When he pushes his hands downward instead of to the sides, I can't help the gasp that escapes me. My nipples tingle, and ripples of pleasure run from wherever he touches me, spread inside me, as my body betrays me shamefully.

It's the same sensuous game as with my thighs.

He comes so close. So close. Every stroke, a little closer. His fingers slide along the soft roundness, then he pauses, just north of my nipples before he moves up again.

I can't help arching to meet his touch, then I remind myself to lie still as per his orders.

And then it happens.

A light brush over each nipple.

All air rushes out of me.

He has to notice how my heart slams beneath his palms.

Up, down, fingers brushing my nipples, then his hands slide along the sides of my chest before they move up again in a circular pattern. On one downward stroke, he catches my hard peaks between his fingers in a firm pinch before he immediately continues down and out.

He removes his hands. I hear his soft steps, then the towel comes up to cover my chest.

I groan inwardly. I'm so unsatisfied, so aroused. This is the best freaking massage I've ever had.

I'm beginning to understand the 'Taboo' part of the name. This is hardly allowed. Probably not in Europe either.

More oil squirting in hands. Then his hands on my feet.

My god, this man knows how to give a foot massage. I

almost forget the burning arousal as I lose myself in the calming pleasure of getting my feet kneaded.

Then, one hand on each shin, sliding up, up, past my knee, along the front of my thigh, all the way up to connect with my pussy, where he lingers a moment.

I jerk and tense up from head to toe.

"Relax, Miss Carmichael," he says in a low, soothing voice.

I shiver as I try to lie heavy on the bench.

He moves to my feet again, moves upward, a firm grip, thumbs pushing against my nether lips again. This time he circles them once before he returns to my feet.

I spread my legs a tiny, tiny bit, needing more, wanting to give him better access.

Christ! Touch me more!

Thumbs, pushing, sliding along my folds, dipping in to rest at my aching entrance before he removes them again.

I whimper.

"Not a sound," he says sternly.

His hands move faster up along my trembling legs, his thumbs breach my opening, pushing inside, deep, rough.

I arch and cry out, my hands gripping the sides of the table.

He leaves one hand there, thumb lodged in my pussy, his hand pushing against my clit, the other hand moving up to my throat, holding me down.

I gasp and look up at him, my heart bolting. He holds my gaze and doesn't look murderous at all. He looks as serene as before, and a little stern.

"Close your eyes, Miss Carmichael."

"I—"

He clenches my throat tighter while moving his thumb inside me, in, out.

On every instroke, he rubs my clit. His hand on my throat, my vulnerability, the feeling of being powerless, and his insistent thrusting in my pussy sends a flood of heat through my body—aching, scorching heat.

I squeeze my eyes shut, hoping this will end well. As in *well*. Hoping I won't end up dying in my orgasmic bliss because he turns out to be a homicidal maniac with really clever hands.

My friend got out, didn't she? It'll be all right.

I hope.

I can breathe, but the pressure on my throat builds pressure between my legs, and the heat between my legs spreads through my belly, to my nipples, to my scorched cheeks.

"Spread your legs."

"What kind of—massage is—this?" I stutter. I can barely form words.

"Deep."

I'll say.

His voice is deep.

His touch is deep.

His thumb in my pussy... *deep*.

I arch up as he moves deeper, faster. He rearranges his hand so his thumb rubs my clit, and it's his fingers that thrust inside instead.

He is right there, right where I need him. The onslaught of sensations—the restraint he's put on me, how helpless I am, the forbidden act—make tension rise and center between my legs. My belly tingles, the insides of my thighs tingle. I'm so close. So, so—

I'm riding the wave of being almost there, on the brink of falling over, when he stops and pulls out.

I moan in disappointment. "Mmmnoo."

"Turn over. Stand on your knees. Chest flat against the mattress. Ass up."

I tremble, but I manage without falling off. Is he going to fuck me now? Here? I'm so fucking ready.

"Knees wider apart."

I shuffle.

"Wider."

I shuffle a little further.

A hard slap on my ass. "Wider."

I squeal as the shockwave rocks through me. "I *can't*. I'll fall off."

"No, you won't. Wider."

I move my knees as far as they go. A little further and they'll slide off. I'm stretchy, but maybe not dive into split-stretchy. I hope he'll be satisfied.

"Good girl," he rumbles, his accent a little more pronounced and insanely sexy.

I close my eyes. It's silent. I have no idea what he's doing. My pussy throbs, and I want him to do *something*. Anything. Soon.

A pleasantly warm liquid trickles between my ass cheeks, dribbles along the insides of my thighs. A sharp scent of herbs fills my nostrils.

Touch me!

His hand on the small of my back holds me in place,

then something hard, not cock hard, but object hard, pushes at my butt hole.

I gasp and clench but I'm not in control here. All the oil makes me helpless as he pushes something unyielding past my tight muscle. It's thick, but it gets worse. It's as if it keeps growing, opening me wider and wider.

"Jesus," I squeal. "I can't!"

He holds still for a few moments.

I sense we're at the peak of its width, and he has stopped right where it stretches me the most.

It's incredibly uncomfortable, and it burns, a burn that leaks into my pussy.

I whimper and pant, trying to breathe through it. Then my body slowly adapts, and as I relax, bit by bit, he moves the plug, or whatever he's pushed inside, a little out, a little in, tiny moves, making the ache flare up over and over. His other hand fingers my clit, and I twitch. Hard.

I'm gonna come. *Now.* I can't hold back.

He removes his hand and pushes the plug all the way in. It's sucked inside and settles there, thick and probing.

I'm so, *so* close, and I groan in disappointment from the lack of completion.

More liquid. This time hotter, poured along my back, pooling between my shoulder blades, then forming two stinging rivers on either side of my nape.

It has another kind of herbal smell than the other oil, and as I sniff it in, I'm overcome by sudden drowsiness.

I'm not sleepy. It's not that.

On the contrary, I'm hyper aware of every sound, smell, touch, but I'm so relaxed I don't think I can ever move again.

"You will not come until I allow you. I will give you pleasure. I will feast on your lust, and all your orgasms from today belong to me."

I don't understand, but at the same time it kind of makes some weird sense. I know it's true. I feel it in my very bones. My body will obey his command.

Now.

Always.

The room seems even hotter and somehow darker. The oil still stings my back. The scents make my head spin. My ass burns. My pussy throbs. It's as if something inside me undulates, squirms, and comes to life. It's frightening and liberating.

My back stopped hurting a long time ago. My every muscle is soft, ready, waiting for whatever comes next. I'm a mindless rag doll and a hyper aware pinpoint of focus and desire, all at once.

Every sense has honed in on Hans. I know where he is even without looking or without listening. I *sense*.

It should freak me out, but it doesn't. It's amazing, like the universe has opened before me.

All this after some incense, a little massage, and a butt plug.

A little voice at the back of my head whimpers 'danger', but I silence it with ease.

I. Am.

"Open yourself to me."

"I have," I whisper.

He inhales, exhales. "I feel it."

I do, too.

He strokes along my back, grabs my hair in his fist, a

hand on my throat, pulling me up, while he pushes me down.

I focus on breathing while thrills shoot through me from wherever he touches me, wherever he applies pressure.

"Keep your head down and your eyes closed at all times. Do not open them again until I tell you."

"I will."

"And no speaking. You may scream."

I gulp and nod.

He cups my breasts, pinching my nipples to the threshold between sweet pain turning torturous, then he slides one hand down my belly, down to cup my pussy while his other hand strokes my back and finds my ass again where he pulls out the plug, almost all the way, jams it inside, pulls it out, eliciting squeals from my throat that I'm in no control of.

Finally, he pulls it out all the way with a little plop, replacing it with his fingers, several fingers from the feel of it, hovering at the entrance. He thrusts inside, breaching both pussy and ass at the same time, making me twitch from the shock of the sudden intrusion, but then I push back, needy like a bitch in heat.

The pressure on my nipples remains the same—on the brink of too much, but not quite there. He must have clamped them. I missed how he did that so seamlessly.

His relentless thrusts, the nipple torture, and the flames that run through me inch me closer and closer, my release almost within reach.

I shake and sweat, my thighs barely hold me up, but I don't dare to move, and I don't want him to stop what he's doing.

I've never been this close without falling over, I've never been tortured with orgasm denial. It's heaven and hell at the same time.

Mostly hell.

I ache, literally *ache*, the tingles between my legs louder, more insistent, almost making me cramp.

"Please." My voice is hoarse, barely there.

Pain shoots along my spine, making the hair rise on my nape and my nipples sting infinitely more. It's over as fast as it started.

"Next time more," he says. "Do not talk."

I swallow. Swallow again. I want to beg. I need to come. Or for the ache to ease up. Anything but this constant tease. The onslaught of non-stop tingling makes my head swim, and even though I don't look up, I feel the room spinning, faster and faster.

I almost beg again, but then I clench my teeth and fight myself.

He breathes heavily, inhales, exhales.

I breathe with him at the same pace, getting light-headed.

Listening to him is almost as arousing as his touch.

I thank the powers that be when he finally climbs up behind me. The mattress sinks down a little, then the head of his cock pushes inside my pussy, stretches me terrifyingly wide. I don't go that wide.

Something is wrong, horribly wrong. No human man is built like that. Still... while he widens me beyond what should be possible, going deeper and deeper, with his fingers thrusting in my ass, the intense rubbing on my clit, the rhythmic pinching of my nipples that feels so much as if his fingers are still there, the spiraling pleasure makes me soar.

I float above my body. His hands are everywhere. It's not fingers in my ass. It's a cock. His cock.

His *cocks* are in me.

Cocks!

His hands, on my hips, on my breasts, in my hair, holding me down, stroking my clit.

Jesus, how they stroke my clit!

I can't breathe.

His eyes glow.

His face has transformed.

He looks cruel, dangerous, as if he devours me.

I do feel increasingly drained. He fucks me with abandon, and I think he's fucking me to death.

Something pushes at my mouth, spreads my lips wide open, and pushes between my teeth. The shock snaps me back into my body, into darkness.

I try to open my eyes, but I can't. The thing in my mouth—feeling strangely much like something organic—like a thick, hot... cock, tasting slightly salty, deliciously spicy, pushes deeper, fills my mouth, stretches my throat, closes my airway on the instroke, pulls out just as I panic and retch, then pushes in again.

I'm stuffed. All my holes are shamefully stretched, used and abused.

That sense of lethargy and lightness overcomes me again, but I stay rooted in my body this time. There's no getting away. My every limb aches, my pussy, ass and throat burn.

Hans groans, louder, rougher until it sounds like snarls

from a beast. The growls he emits don't sound human, and I shudder as I try to remember what I saw.

He's not human. He can't be.

How?

I don't know how long he fucks me, or how deep he goes. I don't know if he hurts me or if I like it. It's both thrilling and scary.

He grunts, stabs his cocks inside me, over, and over, and over. I'm raw and exhausted, my orgasm constantly hovering right out of reach. It's as if he feeds me and feeds *on* me. I can't explain it. I don't dare to even try.

Pace increased beyond what should be possible, he suddenly puts his mouth to my ear.

"You may come now. It will give me great pleasure to feel you give in to me."

I only hear what I need to hear.

Come.

His words send me into forceful convulsions, the spasms wracking my body as I come over and over. My pussy clenches around his pistoning cock, and I jolt up, jerking and twisting, afraid I'll fall off the bed.

He holds my hips in a vice grip, slams into me one last time and roars. His booming voice fills the room and takes over my head. It's as if he milks me of energy, throwing my poor but blissfully happy body into one orgasm after the other.

Finally, we both go still.

It's so silent all of a sudden that all I hear are my own breaths and heartbeats. I turn my head, finally able to open my eyes again.

Hans stands next to me, dressed in his pristine white

pants and shirt, arms rolled up, showing off the intricate tattoos on his forearms, a snake-like pattern slithering along his ropey muscles.

He strokes my back soothingly, back and forth, his hand warm and strong. "You fell asleep, Miss. Your hour has passed. You should feel better now. I have worked on you quite a bit. You were very tense."

I dart up and scan my body frantically. The towel falls to the floor as I move.

I'm naked. I remember he removed my panties. I should be bruised, and sticky, and *icky*, but there is nothing out of the ordinary.

Heat creeps up my cheeks. Did I really dream it?
That?

I glance shyly at him. He's hot as hell. Did I make up the whole thing in my zoned-out, sex-starved mind?

Thinking about three cocks, and I don't know *how* many hands, I realize that of course I did.

"Did... did I snore?"

He gives me a secretive smile. "A gentleman never tells."

Hans turns toward the shelf behind him and hands me a fresh towel that I wrap around me.

I snored. For sure.

I swing my legs over the side of the massage table, surprised at how invigorated I feel. And *relaaaxed*. I haven't felt so nimble and at ease in years.

"How much do I owe you?"

His smile widens, showing too many white teeth for comfort. "This one is on me. Good day, Miss Carmichael. I hope to see you again."

And then he leaves.

I tilt my head from side to side, looking for strained muscles, but I'm amazingly loose, in the best way.

Invigorated and exhilarated, I jump off the table and grab my clothes, stealing glances at the curtain behind which he disappeared. I'm curious about him. Maybe I will come back. My co-worker did *good*, recommending this place to me.

* * *

That night, I have an itch I can't seem to scratch. Maybe it's the massage oil? My skin feels tight, and there's a slight burn, as if I've gotten too much sun.

I go to bed, but the longer I lie, the more my skin stings.

I twist and turn. The stinging pools between my legs, and I pull up the erotic dream from the depths of my subconscious mind as I finger myself.

Nothing.

I'm turned on, but nothing happens. I don't get any closer to release.

I push a finger inside my pussy, then another into my ass. I bury my face in my pillow and try to deny myself air, anything to get off.

But nothing.

The burn between my legs spreads along my back, up to my neck, feeling oddly much like the sensation when Hans poured the hot oil on me.

In my dream, of course.

Something moves under my fingers.

I pull out, horrified, then I touch my pussy again, but feel only my own juices.

As I decide I imagined it, it moves again, in the small of my back, then up my spine.

I dart up and dash to the full-length mirror, twisting, trying to look at my back.

A huge tattoo of a snake, like the one on the wall in the waiting room, *moves* on my skin. It moves! The head part closes around my neck and squeezes.

I clutch at my throat, but there is nothing but my own skin.

The tail part disappears in between my legs, pokes and prods and then pushes inside my pussy, deep, squirmy. It's thick, and alive, and I think I'm going to die. I can barely get air and my heart hammers an aching staccato.

But—

The orgasm looms. Close. Closer. Thick, stretching, tight around my throat, tensing every muscle.

"Hans," I moan. "Please!"

Somehow, I know I have to beg. I need him to allow me.

The snake thrusts even deeper, and then Hans's approval fills me. I exhale in relief and scream and cry as the orgasms wash over me.

* * *

I jerk awake from the alarm. It's six in the morning, and time to get up.

Something is different.

I'm sticky and wet between my legs. My heart skips when I remember the snake, my orgasms, the feeling of

Hans inside, as if he was draining me, feeding off my releases.

I shoot up and look at my back in the mirror, seeing nothing.

At work I smile at my friend. "I went."

"Did you enjoy it?"

I open my mouth. Close it again. Nod. "I'm very... relaxed."

The snake moves under my skin. I don't see the tattoo in daylight, but when the night comes, it pulls me into its tight, slithering grip.

I need it desperately, I hate it even more, and I'll never be free.

Also by Nicolina Martin

NICOLINA MARTIN lives with her daughters, her kitties, (and her dust bunnies...) in a little house on the Swedish west coast. She escapes the long, dark winter nights by writing naughty romance with morally gray heroes, strong heroines, and all the feels.

* * *

Possessive Protectors:

- **Punishing Penelope**
- **Commanding Casey**
- **Saving Sandra**
- **Restraining Reeba**

Russo Saga:

- **Heat**
- **Ruin**
- **Shame**
- **Redemption**
- **Absolution**
- **Capo**

Standalones:

- **Mortem**
- **I Am Eve**
- **Sugar Princess**
- **Break My Chains**

- **<u>Anomaly</u>**
- **<u>Her Vampire Hero</u>**

Pure filth...

- **<u>Honey Trap</u>**
- **<u>Firefighter's Pet</u>**
- **<u>Demon Lust</u>**

For everything Nicolina

BOOKS, SOCIALS, ETC

linktr.ee/nicolinamartin

Acknowledgments

Thank you my wonderful editor, Nerine Dorman.

www.ingramcontent.com/pod-product-compliance
Lightning Source LLC
LaVergne TN
LVHW092026190726
843493LV00002B/605